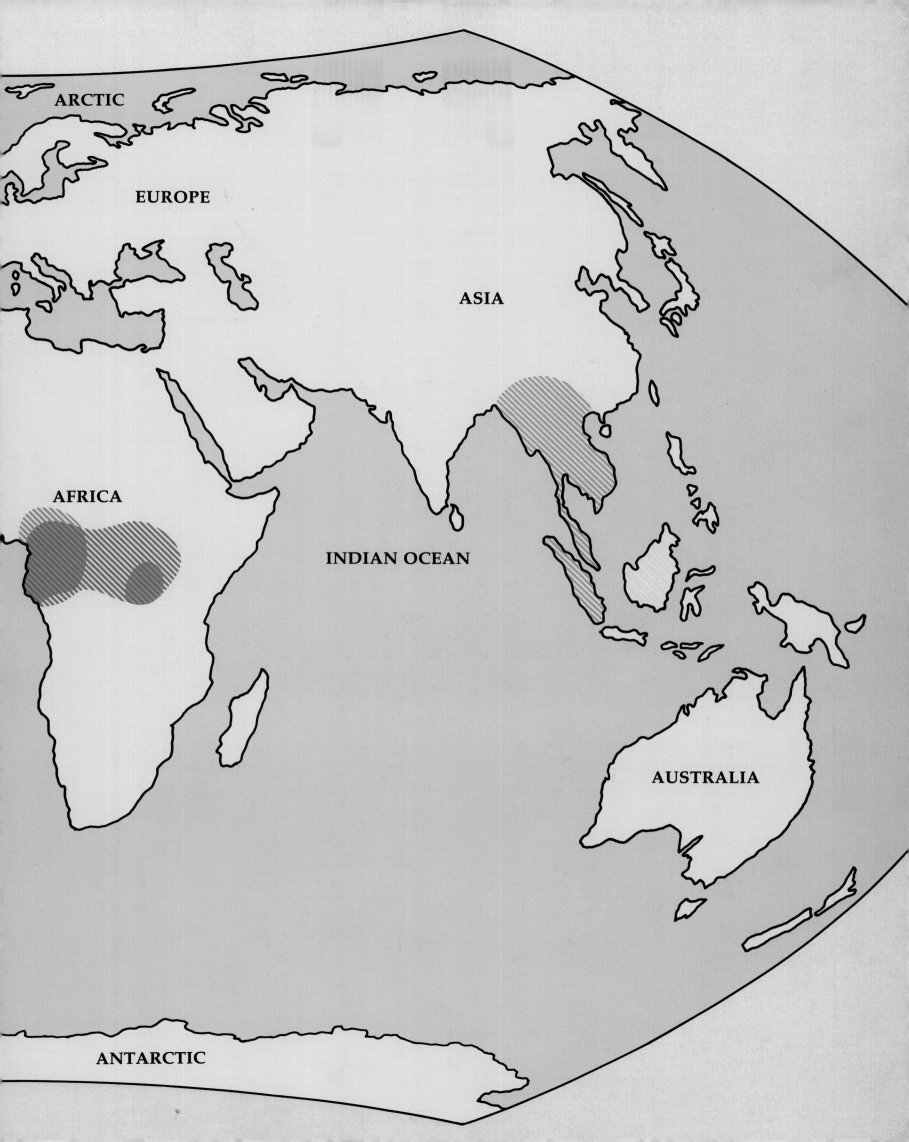

For Shirley and Cyril
T. L.

For Alain, the artiste
J. B.

Text copyright © 1993 by Tess Lemmon
Illustrations copyright © 1993 by John Butler
First American edition 1993 published by Ticknor & Fields,
A Houghton Mifflin company, 215 Park Avenue South, New York, New York 10003.
First published in Great Britain by David Bennett Books Ltd.

Manufactured in Singapore.

Book design by Roger Hands & John Butler
Text of this book is set in Palatino.
The illustrations are acrylic.

10 9 8 7 6 5 4 3 2 1

The author of this book both loved monkeys and apes and understood them. Tess Lemmon worked with woolly monkeys, at the Woolly Monkey Sanctuary in Cornwall. She then went to the Gambia, in Africa, where she helped look after orphaned chimpanzees, and for a year took care of Polly, a baby baboon, whom she successfully reintroduced into baboon society. Tess was caring and sensitive, but also brave enough to stand up for what she believed. She championed the cause of monkeys and apes, by working for the International Primate Protection League and supporting organizations such as the Jane Goodall Foundation, and also by using her skills as a writer to expose in print those who continue to abuse primates.

Library of Congress Cataloging-in-Publication Data

Lemmon, Tess.
    Apes / written by Tess Lemmon ; illustrated by John Butler. —
1st American ed.
     p.   cm.
    Summary: Describes the physical characteristics, habits, and
behavior of the members of the ape family: gorillas, chimpanzees,
orangutans, and gibbons.
  ISBN 0-395-66901-4
    1. Apes—Juvenile literature. [1. Apes.] I. Butler, John,
1952-   ill. II. Title.
QL737.P96L445 1993
599.88—dc20   92-37692
                                     CIP
                                     AC

APES

Written by
TESS LEMMON

Illustrated by
JOHN BUTLER

TICKNOR & FIELDS
NEW YORK
1993

CONTENTS

gorilla
(*Gorilla gorilla*)

orangutan
(*Pongo pygmaeus*)

male
Height: 5.5 feet
Weight: 310-400 pounds

female
Height: 5 feet
Weight: 200 pounds

male
Head & body: 3 feet
Weight: 130-200 pounds

Gibbons

Gorillas

Conservation

Protecting apes

Although other apes are measured by the length of their head and body, gorillas are always measured by their height when standing up.

chimpanzee
(*Pan troglodytes*)

gibbon (lar gibbon)
(*Hylobates lar*)

female	*male*	*female*	*male*	*female*
Head & body: 2.5 feet	Head & body: 2.5-3 feet	Head & body: 2.25-2.75 feet	Head & body: 1.5-2 feet	Head & body: 1.5-2 feet
Weight: 90-110 pounds	Weight: 90 pounds	Weight: 65 pounds	Weight: 12.6 pounds	Weight: 11.7 pounds

Introduction

Gorillas, chimpanzees, orangutans, and gibbons are all apes. Apes, human beings, and monkeys are closely related, and belong to a group of animals called primates. Instead of hooves or paws, primates have hands and feet that can hold and grasp. Gibbons are called lesser apes because they are smaller than the others, which are called great apes. All apes are forest-dwellers, and they eat mainly fruit, leaves, and insects.

Over millions of years, primates evolved from a mouselike creature that once lived in trees.

The easiest way to tell an ape from a monkey is to remember that apes do not have tails.

An ape's arms are longer than its legs. In trees, monkeys run along branches on all fours, but apes hold their bodies upright and swing by their arms beneath the branches. This is why apes have developed such long, strong arms, and why they do not need tails to help them balance or grip.

On the ground, chimpanzees, gorillas, and orangutans use their strong arms to take their weight as they walk.

An ape's hands and feet look like human hands. Its feet each have a big toe which is separate from the other four toes and looks like a thumb. When apes climb trees they can grasp branches with their hands *and* their feet.

An ape's hands are so nimble that it can pick fruit and leaves with its fingers, and even snatch insects out of the air.

Apes rely on their eyesight far more than their sense of smell, so their noses are small.

Orangutans and chimpanzees can hold fruit in their feet as well as in their hands.

All apes are active during the day. Unlike many animals, apes have eyes that face forward, so they can see clearly where they are going as they move through the trees. They have excellent eyesight, and can see in color, unlike some animals which see only in black and white. Color vision helps them see when fruit is ready to eat: many unripe fruits are green but turn yellow or red when ripe.

Some apes live alone or in twos and threes; others live in groups of fifty or more. They spend their days looking for food, eating, resting, and being with each other.

The great apes are too big to be killed and eaten by most animals. Sometimes a lion, leopard, or snake snatches a young ape that has strayed from its mother, but this does not happen often. The lesser apes are hard to catch because they live so high in the trees.

Grooming one another is one way in which apes show affection. It helps to strengthen relationships between friends and members of the same family. Two apes take turns combing through each other's hair with their fingers to get rid of dry skin and dirt. This is so relaxing that sometimes the ape being groomed falls asleep.

Apes usually have one baby at a time. The mother suckles and carries her baby for several years, so she could not manage more than one at a time.

Apes that live together get to know each other very well. They experience many different moods, including annoyance, curiosity, and contentment. They express how they feel by the look on their faces, the way they move their bodies, and the sounds they make, so one ape can easily tell the mood of another.

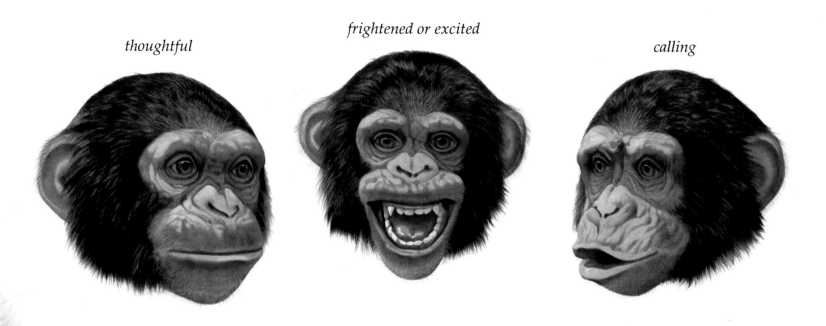

thoughtful

frightened or excited

calling

Apes have a long childhood. Some are not grown up until they are fifteen years old. A young ape needs time to learn how to look after itself in the forest, and how to behave properly—being polite to its elders, for instance. It learns by watching its mother and other adults, and is scolded for wrongdoings. Punishments include being screamed at or bitten.

At night, most apes make nests in the trees or on the ground. They bend and intertwine leafy branches, then pile more leaves and branches on top. This makes a springy mat that is both comfortable and warm— for the forest can get chilly at night.

11

Orangutans

Orangutans are the world's largest tree-living mammals. They live in the hot jungles of Borneo and Sumatra, two islands in Southeast Asia.

The people who live there have a legend that the orangutan was once a man who did wrong, and fled to the jungle to escape being punished. Orangutan means "man of the forest."

Orangs climb around very slowly and carefully because they are so heavy. They spread their weight across the branches by grasping with their hands and feet. Their feet are so much like hands that it is as if they have four hands. Even so, they sometimes make mistakes and come crashing down to the ground. Many orangs break their arms or legs in accidents, but these usually heal.

Too big to leap from one tree to the next, the orang has found other ways of traveling in the trees. Sometimes it can stretch across with its long arms, or else it rocks the tree it is in until the tree bends over and makes a bridge. If this is unsuccessful, the orang goes to the ground.

An orang walks on all fours, using either the palms of its hands or its fists. Big males travel on the ground more often than females and young orangs, because the trees cannot always bear their weight.

During the monsoon season in Borneo and Sumatra, rain pours down for several hours every day, and the orangutans can get soaked to the skin. They do not like getting wet, and try to take shelter under leaves. Sometimes an orang breaks off a huge leaf to use as an umbrella.

The orang's long, shaggy hair comes in handy when it is thirsty. It dips its arm into the puddles that collect in tree holes, and sucks the drops from its hair.

Unlike other kinds of apes, orangutans spend most of their time alone. Because of their size, they need to eat a great deal of food every day to stay alive. If too many of them lived together in the same area of the jungle, the food would soon be used up.

Young orangs enjoy playing games.

Males and females come together to mate, but then the male goes away again. A female has her first baby between seven and ten years old, and is not ready to mate again for about three years.

The female looks after the baby entirely on her own. For the first year of its life, the baby clings constantly to her chest or back, but after that it follows her around. By this time, it is eating solid food, but it continues to be suckled for about three years. When it is about four years old, its mother may have another baby, but the older child does not leave her until it is adult, when it is about seven years old.

If adult females meet at the same tree they ignore each other, eat, and go their separate ways. However, young orangs are much more outgoing than adults, and they play together while their mothers eat. They wrestle and tumble around, and climb all over each other.

Male orangutans avoid one another by calling to announce their presence. Males call mostly when they get up in the morning and just before they go to sleep. The sound starts as a grumble and builds up to a roar that can be heard over a mile away—which is why scientists named it the "long call." When one male hears another, he goes in the opposite direction.

Bees, honey, ants, and leaves are all part of an orang's diet, but mostly orangs eat fruit such as mangoes, durians, and lychees. In the rain forest, different trees bear fruit at different times of the year, so orangs need to know where and when to look for food. Fortunately, they can remember not only where a particular tree is, but also when it has fruit.

The males of Sumatra have smaller cheek flaps than the males of Borneo.

The face of an adult male orangutan looks nothing like a baby orang's face. The baby's face is flat and resembles a human baby's. The male has a beard and flaps of skin on each side of his face.

Sumatran male orangutan

Bornean males have short mustaches, and they have darker hair and rounder heads than Sumatran males.

Each male has a pouch of skin at his throat, which he fills with air to make his voice even louder. The pouch looks like an enormous double chin when it is empty.

Bornean male orangutan

Chimpanzees

Chimpanzees live in the forests of eastern, western, and central Africa. Some of these forests are thick, tangled tropical rain forests. Others are open woodlands, with patches of grassland. Chimpanzees generally travel on the ground, but climb trees to find fruit and leaves to eat, or to chase prey.

Big ears help chimpanzees to hear well. When chimps are out of each other's sight in the forest they hoot to keep in contact.

Up to 120 chimpanzees live together in a community. Usually, one part of the forest cannot provide enough food for all of them, so the chimps divide into smaller groups to feed. Males often go with each other, and females go with their offspring. Sometimes the whole community will feast together on a tree laden with fruit.

In the past, scientists believed that human beings were the only animals clever enough to use tools, but now we know that chimpanzees use tools such as sticks or stones, too. When picking a stone to crack open a nut, a chimp must choose carefully. The stone has to be heavy enough to break the shell, but not so heavy that it squashes the kernel.

When they are on the ground, chimpanzees walk on all fours. This is called knuckle-walking, because they put the backs of their fingers and knuckles against the ground.

Chimpanzees regularly eat insects, monkeys, and antelope. Monkeys are hard to catch because they escape through the trees, so five or six chimps may hunt them together. They surround a troop of monkeys, then part of the group picks out a single monkey and chases it toward the others, who are waiting to catch it. Sometimes the monkeys scream at the chimps and chase them away.

Chimpanzees can live for as long as forty or fifty years.

Elderly chimps sometimes go gray or become bald.

Deep in the forests of Zaire, in central Africa, lives an animal so closely related to chimpanzees that when it was first discovered, it was called the pygmy chimpanzee. It is now named the bonobo, after a town in Zaire.

The bonobo is much the same size as the chimpanzee; however, it is lighter in build and more graceful. The bonobo has smaller ears than the chimpanzee, a central part in its hair, and long sideburns. A bonobo's life is very similar to that of a chimpanzee.

17

All the chimpanzees in one community know one another very well. Mothers have a strong bond with their children, and many nonrelated chimps form close friendships. Within a community, some chimps are dominant over the others. They take the best food, and the other chimps show them respect by crouching in front of them when they meet. Adult males are dominant over females. Most arguments occur when young adult males try to become dominant over older ones. Most males stay in the same community all their lives, but grown-up females join another community.

Each community lives in its own area of forest, and groups of males patrol the boundaries of their territory. If they meet chimps from neighboring communities, they try to scare them away by standing up to make themselves look bigger and making their hair stand on end. Then they charge around screaming and throwing branches. If this does not work, they fight.

Hugging, kissing, and back-patting are all ways in which chimpanzees show their affection for one another. Grooming one another is a particularly important expression of friendship.

A female chimpanzee has her first baby when she is about thirteen years old. For its first few months, the baby clings to her hairy chest, but as it becomes heavier, it rides on her back. The mother does not have another baby until the first one starts to look after itself, when it is about five years old. Even when they become adults, between thirteen and fifteen years old, chimpanzees spend much of their time with their mothers.

A young chimp drinks its mother's milk for five years, but begins to eat solid food when it is between three and five months old. Sometimes its mother gives it food, but usually it picks up any scraps she drops, or it chews the other end of whatever she is eating. When it begs for food by putting its mouth near hers, she lets it take bites out of her mouth.

Playing is important, because it helps chimpanzees get to know each other, and it teaches them to control their strength. Young chimps wrestle, tickle each other, and play tug-of-war with sticks. They usually play with their elder brothers and sisters, and their mothers.

Gibbons

Gibbons are the smallest apes. They live in the tropical forests of Southeast Asia, in countries such as Thailand and Malaysia. Since these forests are cut off from each other by seas and rivers, species of gibbon differ greatly from forest to forest.

The pileated gibbon has pale tufts of hair at the side of its head.

The siamang is bigger than any of the others, and almost twice as heavy.

The concolor gibbon has a more pointed head than the others.

Some gibbons are pale yellow, some are jet black, some are silvery gray—and some even change color during their lifetimes! They are born a light color, then turn dark, then light again. In some species, males and females are different colors. For example, the female hoolock gibbon is golden; the male is black.

Gibbons are the acrobats of the ape world. They use their long arms to hang from high branches and swing along at top speed—and when they leap across gaps, they look like they are flying. They swing by holding on, first with one arm, then the other, their long fingers hooking over the branches.

Gibbons cannot walk on all fours because their arms are so much longer than their legs. Instead, they walk upright and hold their arms above their heads to keep them out of the way. Gibbons seldom come to the ground, and, when they stand up in the trees, they look like tightrope-walkers.

Gibbons are the only apes that do not build nests. They sleep sitting up in the forks of branches. They are quite comfortable because they have pads of skin on their backsides which are like built-in cushions.

Gibbons are the only apes to live in pairs, and mate for life. A male and female often have two or three children of different ages living with them. The whole family travels through the trees every day in search of ripe fruit, leaves, and shoots to eat. Gibbons are so small and light that they can hang from the tips of branches and reach fruit growing right at the ends.

Gibbons are the most territorial of the apes, but if one male wants to take over another's territory, they usually manage to settle the dispute without fighting. They try to scare each other by shaking branches and leaping about. Sometimes, two enemies sit face to face in neighboring trees and sing at each other, until one gives up and goes away. A gibbon sings one long, repeated note.

Well-hidden in the leafy treetops, gibbons are more likely to be heard than seen—for the first thing they do when they wake up in the morning is sing. The male starts hooting and whooping, then the female joins in. Their duet lasts at least fifteen minutes. The noise carries far away. When other gibbons hear it, they know they must avoid that part of the forest because it is another family's home.

The siamang has a throat pouch of loose skin that expands with air to the size of its head when it sings. This makes its voice even louder. Some other gibbons have these pouches too, but not such big ones.

22

Female gibbons have a baby every two
or three years. Some father apes do not
take care of their children, but gibbon
fathers groom their children and play
with them. When a siamang baby
is about eight months old, its father
carries it during the day, and hands
it back to its mother at night.

When they are grown up, at eight years old,
gibbons leave their parents to find a mate and
live in their own patch of forest. They break
away gradually, spending more and more time
by themselves. Their parents become more
hostile towards them, and sometimes scream
to make them go away.

Gorillas

Gorillas are the largest apes. They live mostly on the ground because they are too big to live in trees. There are three types of gorilla, and they live in different parts of central Africa.

The western lowland gorilla lives in Cameroon, the Central African Republic, Gabon, Congo, Equatorial Guinea, and Nigeria. The eastern lowland gorilla lives only in eastern Zaire, and the mountain gorilla lives in Rwanda, Uganda, and Zaire—but the two types never meet because the mountain gorilla lives 5,400 to 12,400 feet up the mountains. The mountain gorilla has longer hair to keep it warm in the cold climate.

eastern lowland gorilla

All gorillas live in forests with clearings where the light reaches the ground and helps plants to grow there. Gorillas eat these plants, so they have no trouble finding food. They sit in a clearing and take huge handfuls. Like human beings, they eat only certain parts of different plants: sometimes just the leaves or the stalk or the root. Wild celery, wild ginger, and nettles are some of their favorites. Between meals, gorillas snooze and sunbathe. Resting helps them digest their food.

Plants need a great deal of chewing, so the gorilla has big teeth. It also has very strong jaws that are worked by muscles running all the way from the top of its head. This is why gorillas have big heads.

In order to provide themselves with enough energy, gorillas have to eat enormous meals that last 2 or 3 hours at a time. They start with a big breakfast, have snacks during the day, and eat another meal before going to sleep. An adult male munches through 45 to 65 pounds of greens every day. Gorillas also eat insects and a little fruit.

Even though gorillas are big, they are difficult to see when they sit in the undergrowth. A person or animal could walk right past them without knowing they were there. Sometimes their voices give them away. While they eat, they smack their lips and grunt with enjoyment.

Gorillas live in groups of about twelve animals. Each group is made up of several adult females and their young, plus at least one adult male.

The biggest adult male is the leader of the group. When he starts walking, everyone else follows him. When he sits down, the others sit too. He is called a silverback, because the hair on his back is a silver color. Young males whose hair has not yet changed color are called blackbacks.

The silverback is big and strong, but also very gentle. Young gorillas play with him by jumping on his head or pulling his hair, but he does not seem to mind at all. If he gets tired of it he just stares at them, and that makes them stop.

A new-born gorilla is only about half the size of a new-born human baby. Snuggling in its mother's hair, a baby gorilla is almost invisible.

When it is about two months old, a baby gorilla starts to crawl. At eight to nine months old it can walk, but it continues taking rides on its mother's back until it is three or four years old. Gorillas stay close to their mothers until they are grown up, at about ten years old. Most adult gorillas leave the group to find mates and start groups of their own.

A gorilla group keeps together all the time, whether resting, traveling, or eating. Any gorilla that loses sight of the group makes little grunting sounds to let the others know where it is.

When they play with each other, young gorillas get so excited that they stand upright and beat their chests. Adults beat their chests only when they are angry or worried—for example, when they hear an odd sound, or suddenly see a buffalo or an elephant. The silverback beats his chest when he meets other gorillas, as a warning to tell the strangers to go away. Gorillas seldom fight.

Conservation

For thousands of years, apes have been living in their forest homes. Now, because of people who kill or capture them, and destroy their habitats, apes are in danger of becoming extinct.

The biggest threat to all apes is the destruction of their habitat, without which they cannot survive. People have always cut down trees to make space for themselves, but now there are more and more people in the world, needing more and more space. Forests are being replaced by houses or fields for food crops.

Chimpanzees

Baby chimps are kept as pets in Africa and abroad. They are also smuggled into Spain, where they are dressed up and used by photographers who take pictures of people holding them. They are drugged to keep them quiet, and the clothes make their hair fall out. Most of them die within a few months.

Orangutans

There are more orangutans living in the modern city of Taipei on Taiwan, than in the jungles where they belong. It is fashionable in Taipei to keep them as pets, but they are often abandoned, and found wandering around shopping centers. Orangs are also kept as pets or performing animals in other countries, including the United States.

Gibbons

Baby gibbons are kept in tiny cages in local markets and sold as pets. Many die from starvation and neglect. Some gibbons (and chimpanzees) are sold to scientists abroad, who carry out experiments on them. Apes are so much like humans that they can be used to test drugs, for example.

Gorillas

The mountain gorilla is one of the most endangered animals in the world. There are only a few hundred of them left. Hunters used to kill gorillas and sell their hands and heads as souvenirs. They are now protected by armed guards who patrol the forests, but they are still in danger. Gorillas get caught in traps that hunters have set to catch antelope. Lowland gorillas are also captured for sale to zoos.

Protecting apes

Although apes are often mistreated and some types are in danger of extinction, people from all over the world are working to protect them. Some of these people work in the parts of the world where apes still live in the wild, protecting them from poachers, studying their behavior, and working with the people who live there to save the apes and their habitats.

When she saw baby monkeys stacked up in cages at an airport, Dr. Shirley McGreal set up the International Primate Protection League (IPPL), to help all primates. IPPL, with offices all over the world, tracks down illegal animal dealers and runs a sanctuary for ex-laboratory gibbons in Summerville, S.C. It also supports Chimfunshi Wildlife Orphanage, in Zambia, Africa, which looks after chimps that have been rescued from beach photographers or laboratories and those that have been pets but have grown too difficult for their owners to look after. Dr. McGreal says that she tries to say and do what primates would if they were able to speak and act for themselves.

There are also organizations which protect gorillas. Dian Fossey created the Mountain Gorilla Fund to raise money to protect the remaining 600 mountain gorillas. She lived with one particular group of gorillas in the forest high in the Virunga Mountains in Central Africa. These gorillas, and Dian Fossey's work with them, are the subject of a well-known book, *Gorillas in the Mist*, which was later made into a film.

Jane Goodall, who has been studying chimps for 30 years, has recently set up the Jane Goodall Institute (JGI) to protect chimps everywhere. JGI tries to assure humane treatment for all chimps, including those in zoos and those being used for medical research. JGI also runs sanctuaries in Africa in Uganda, Congo, and Burundi.

All these people and many others dedicate much of their lives to making sure that all apes are protected and given the best possible chance to survive.